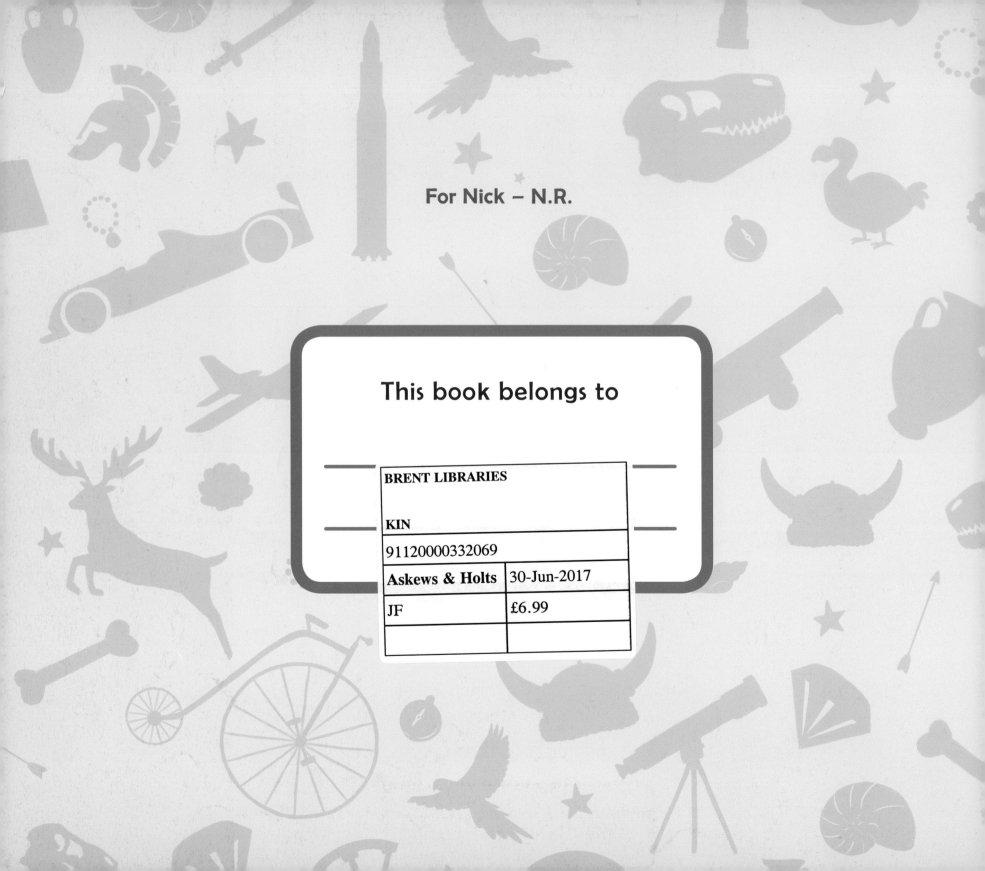

For Nick – N.R.

This book belongs to

Max & Zap
at the
Museum

Illustrated by Natasha Rimmington

Picture Kelpies

Max dragged his mum and little sister
down the busy street and squeezed into
the spinning door.
PUSH...
Today they were visiting his favourite
place – **THE MUSEUM**.

SUMMER EXHIBITION

Entrance

He didn't know it yet, but Max was about to have an extremely exciting, supremely special adventure.

UP... UP... UP...

in the lift they zoomed.

Max raced past his **VERY SLOW** little sister towards his favourite room – with armour, cannons and swords.

"I haven't seen that shiny armour before, Zap,"
Max told his toy robot.
He picked up the armour, squeezed it over his head...

...and came face to face with a **REAL, LIVING** clan chief! With a **REAL, VERY SHARP** sword! Max leapt out of the way and looked around. **THE MUSEUM HAD COME TO LIFE!**

A grand-looking lady nearby called out,
"COME HERE, YOUNG KNIGHT!"
Max stepped towards her and bowed.

"My name is Mary,
Queen of Scots,"
she said, "and I have
a **QUEST** for you."

"Someone has stolen my precious jewels and left this puzzling clue. Can you help me find them?"
"Yes, your majesty," Max replied.
The Queen unfurled a scroll:

Clue 1

By the objects most old lies the missing gold.

MOST OLD... Max thought very hard.
Suddenly he knew where to look...

ROoOOAAAAAAR!!!

"Dinosaurs are **REALLY OLD**, but I'm not asking that one about the clue!" said Max.

Luckily, the T-rex chased a lion out of the room.
PHEW! Then Max noticed a triceratops. "Excuse me,"
he said, "are you **REALLY OLD?**"
"**HOW RUDE!**" She knocked Max over with her tail.

BOOF!

"I am a mere **68 MILLION** years old!" the triceratops huffed.
"The rocks over there are **BILLIONS** of years older than me."

Then she began to yawn – with **SUPER-STINKY** breath!
Max scrambled to his feet and sprinted to the next room.

"Here are all the rocks, but which one is the oldest?" Max wondered.

1. Ammonite, 90 million years old
2. Amethyst, 130 million years old
3. Meteorite, 4.5 billion years old

"Triceratops was right. Look, we've found the Queen's first missing jewel! And another clue..."

Clue 2

A creature that once lived in Scotland guards a glittering golden band.

Just then Max heard a snuffling sound. He tiptoed towards it...

…and saw a deer the size of a horse, with **ANTLERS** the size of **BRANCHES**.
"Are you lost, pal?" it asked.
"I'm looking for a creature that once lived in Scotland. Can you help me?"

"Climb aboard, and I'll take you to the old forest, wee man."
Max scrambled up and they galloped away, **WHOOSHING** past
fascinating folk from faraway times and places.

Soon, trees reached up all around them.
Max thanked the giant deer, hopped down
and tiptoed along a path that twisted through a
spooky forest. But what was hiding in the trees?

SCOTTISH FOREST,
6000 YEARS AGO

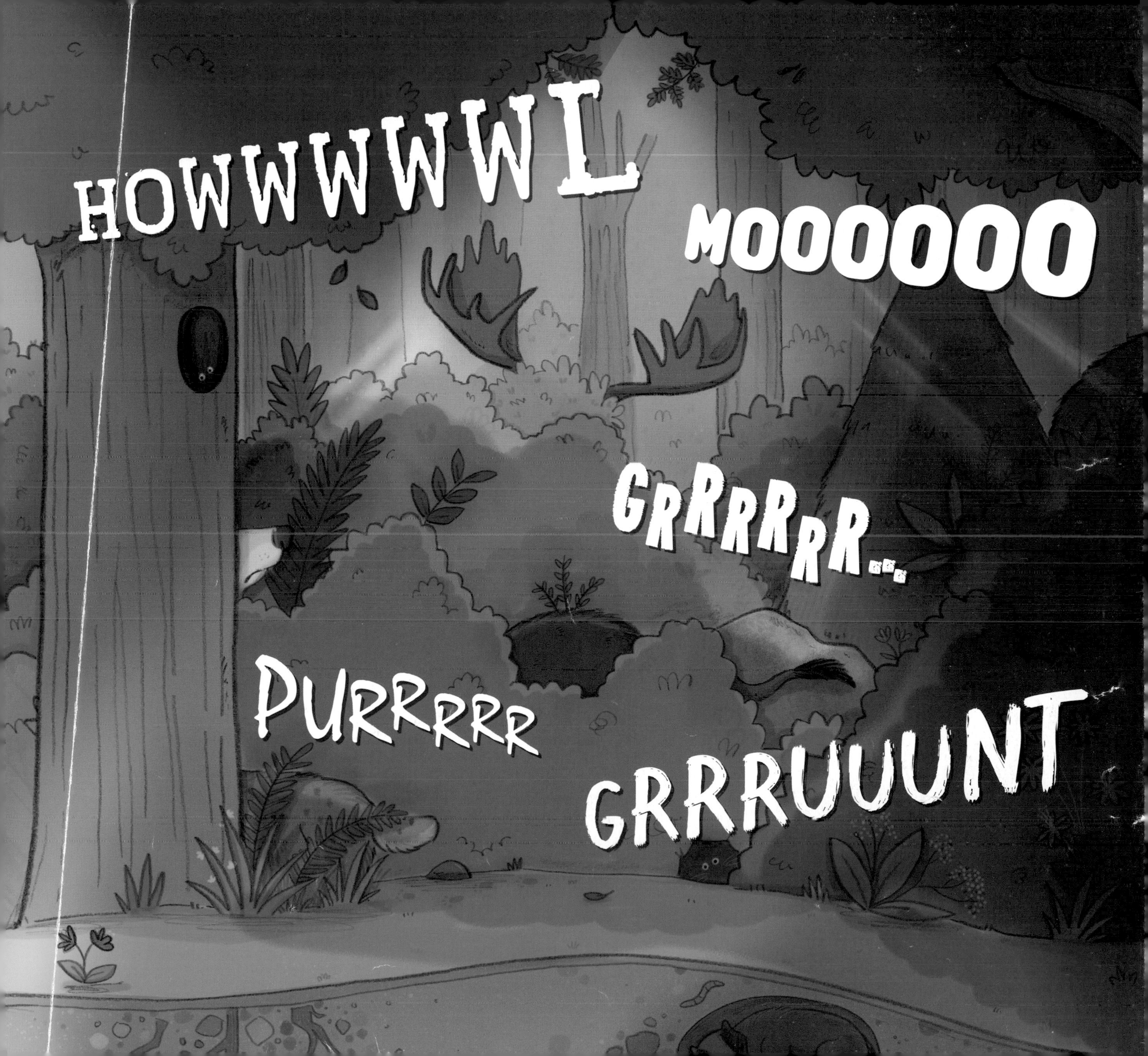
HOWWWWWL
MOOOOOOO
GRRRRRR...
PURRRRR
GRRRUUUNT

Brrr!
Look, an
Arctic fox!

"Excuse me, did you once live in Scotland?" Max asked the friendly fox. "Yes, but I haven't lived here for twelve thousand years." A glittering golden necklace hung from its tail, and nearby was another clue:

Clue 3

Quick! Leave the snow, and zoom as fast as you can go!

Once again, Max knew where to look...

Wheels were turning, pistons pumping, engines whirring. But in this huge room full of vehicles, which one was the fastest?

A motorcycle — pretty fast.

Then Max noticed a hot-air balloon
floating up to the ceiling and back down.

UP... DOWN...

UP... DOWN...

UP...

They leapt on board.

UP...

UP...

THEY SAILED

until Zap reached the
third missing jewel,
and a clue that read:

Clue 4

I stand on a board
of brown and white.
Come and play,
I won't bite!

Once more, Max knew where to look...

The famous **LEWIS CHESSMEN** were in the middle of a match. The Berserker shuffled towards Max. "If you help me win, I'll give you Mary's final jewel."

"How do **YOU** know her jewels are missing?" asked Max.

The chessman winked. **"I STOLE THEM."**

Max was determined to complete his quest.
"What should I do?" he asked.
"Jump diagonally onto the King's row." Max jumped and the King toppled to the ground!

Checkmate!

"I've waited **HUNDREDS OF YEARS** to do that!" said the Berserker. "Thanks for playing with me, Max."

Just then, Mary, Queen of Scots strode towards them. "Was that cheeky chessman behind this prank?" She sighed.

"Yes, your majesty, but look! **I FOUND ALL YOUR JEWELS!**"

"Thank you, young knight, and well done.
Now it's time to say farewell."
"Goodbye, your majesty."
Max waved to his new friends and lifted
the shimmering armour over his head.
The room began to change...

Back in the normal world, Max returned the armour,
no longer shimmering, to the dressing-up box.
   "Hey, Zap," he said. But Zap didn't reply.
He was a toy again.

Then he heard a familiar voice calling, "**MAAAAX!**"
Mum gave him a big hug.

Even after an extremely exciting, supremely special adventure,
it felt good to be back in the everyday world of mums and little sisters.

"Did that **REALLY** just happen?" Max wondered as they walked out of the museum, past the very small, very still Lewis Chessmen…

Then he saw the Berserker **SMILING!**
"**YES!**" Max laughed. "**IT REALLY DID!**"